A wide-eyed Ivrian swam toward her past a row of sculpted lizardfolk standing atop stone columns, his glowing fins briefly tinting them in emerald light. Beyond was the circular light of the pool rim. Heltan had reached it and was already clambering up.

Rendak and Alderra were halfway there, while Kalina held on to the rim, looking back. Jekka hung back, suspended in the water near Rendak, waiting for the oncoming boggards with spear readied.

Then the sea drake appeared, sending a ripple of lightning through the boggards even as it tore through the pack, leaving bloody limbs in its wake. The closest three were caught by the electrical blast.

Along with Ivrian.

Damn it!

As the boy sank, Mirian dove after, knowing it was foolish, that he was probably dead already.

The drake thrashed through the water like a winged eel, set on rending and devouring everything in reach. The remaining boggards scattered, one swimming straight down for Mirian, who paused to blow a smoking hole through its face.

Then she had Ivrian by a shoulder strap and was kicking toward the surface. She saw in surprise that he was kicking feebly himself. The boy was hard to kill.

As she rose, Mirian saw Alderra swimming down, spear in hand, and called for her to get out. But Lady Galanor drove the weapon into a boggard as another gouged her shoulder with a clawed foot. The water was a fury of crazed forms, Kalina and Jekka fighting savagely to keep the path open.

Rendak was suddenly there at her side, grabbing Ivrian's other shoulder strap. With his aid, their speed almost doubled.

The sea drake roared, and the water hummed with another blast of electricity . . .

The Pathfinder Tales Library

Beyond the Pool of Stars

Howard Andrew Jones

A TOM DOHERTY ASSOCIATES BOOK

New York

PATHFINDER TALES: BEYOND THE POOL OF STARS

Maps by Crystal Frasier

A Tor Book
Published by Tom Doherty Associates, LLC
175 Fifth Avenue
New York, NY 10010

www.tor-forge.com

Tor® is a registered trademark of Tom Doherty Associates, LLC.

The Library of Congress Cataloging-in-Publication Data

Jones, Howard A.
    Beyond the pool of stars / Howard Andrew Jones.—First edition.
        p. cm.—(Pathfinder tales)
    "A Tom Doherty Associates Book."
    ISBN 978-0-7653-7453-0 (trade paperback)
    ISBN 978-1-4668-4265-6 (e-book)
I. Title.
    PS3610.O62535 B49 2015
    813'.6—dc23

                                                                2015025412

First Edition: October 2015

Printed in the United States of America

0 9 8 7 6 5 4 3 2 1

In memory of my father, Victor Howard Jones, who showed me to judge individuals on merit rather than appearance, and talked so knowledgeably and lovingly with me about character concept and story structure.

Inner Sea Region

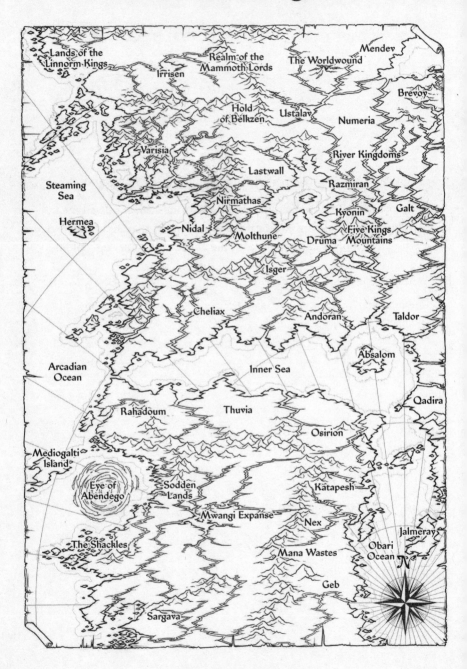

Sargava

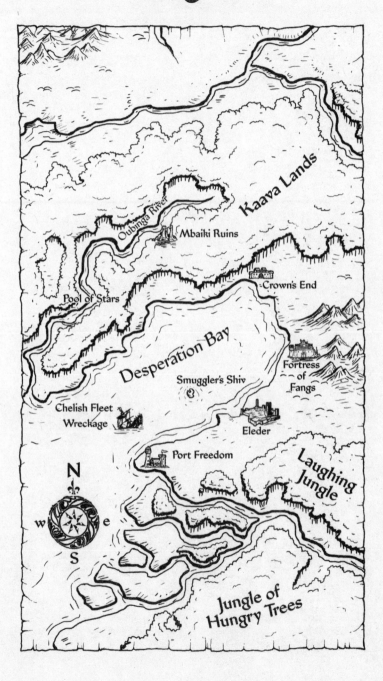

1

Homecoming
Mirian

Every day, dozens of transport ships plied the waters between Sargava's southern port and its capital, Eleder. Stacks of square-cut logs, crates of ivory, and packets of dried medicinal plants came north. Baskets of luxury goods and bright bales of Mulaa cloth went south.

These goods were shepherded by folk who sailed the route several times each week, so accustomed to the trip they scarcely came out from under the sun-bleached awnings or looked up from their deck benches. Although the occasional wanderer, pilgrim, or explorer might admire the rocky surf or the lush coastline, it was rare for the regulars to give much heed to either, and unheard of for them to crowd the rails.

But then, it wasn't every day they saw a pirate ship. When the *Red Leopard*'s lookout cried warning, the passengers surged for a view of the doom to come.

Mirian Raas pushed her way through the throng. Despite the more pressing concerns, muted cries of outrage followed her wake. A pasty colonial woman openly scowled at her.

Mirian ignored them. She reached the *Red Leopard*'s starboard rail with the bulk of the mob to her right. She gripped it tight, searching through the tattered mist hung above the uncharacteristically dull waves. The fog had risen on the heels of afternoon rain, graying the turquoise waters and throwing a smoky curtain across the horizon. It lent a more fearsome aspect to the fast-moving raider astern—a two-master flying a snapping black banner with a sword in a skeletal hand.

Mirian scanned the pirate vessel swiftly, only to have her attention stolen by a startlingly familiar little ship beyond it, just visible through the fog.

The pirate ship had swung out from beyond the bluff, emerging only a quarter league aft, and the other passengers hadn't the wit to see from its trajectory that its target wasn't the *Red Leopard*. Mirian glanced back to the quarterdeck and read the same conclusion in the eyes and activities of the crew there. The raider was aimed for the little caravel flying Mirian's family pennant.

Mirian would have recognized the lines of *The Daughter of the Mist* anywhere, even if the blue flag with a golden swordfish weren't waving from its main mast. The ship's sails were reefed, so Mirian knew the salvagers were below water searching for treasure, her brother Kellic probably leading.

The *Daughter* was swift and nimble when underway, but her crew was about to be caught flat-footed. They didn't stand a chance against the surprise attack.

Not unless . . .

Mirian turned and fought back through the frightened crowd. She'd spent long years inland, but her sea legs were still good, and she had no trouble running the rolling deck once clear. In moments she stood near the wheel and Captain Akimba.

The captain cocked a skeptical eyebrow at her arrival. He was a spare, dark-skinned Ijo man with a blunt nose; he cut a rakish figure with his tricorne hat and well-tended light blue coat. He'd struck Mirian as both perceptive and good-natured as they'd traded pleasantries earlier that day.

She greeted him with a sharp nod. "Captain, we've got to help that ship."

Akimba shook his head. "We can't, Miss Raas."

The stubby helmsman beside him goggled at the notion.

She continued her argument. "Between the *Leopard* and the *Daughter,* we'll have enough men to stop her. I'm sure there's a bounty on that pirate—"

Akimba's mellow voice held little warmth. "You can't know how many that pirate's fielding, or how many are on that caravel."

"Fine. Just get me close, then."

His brows furrowed. "What?"

They were running out of time. Mirian struggled to keep her impatience checked. "Damn it, Captain, tack a few degrees starboard! You'll pass close enough for me to swim for it."

He blinked, dumbfounded, his broad-voweled accent more pronounced. "You want to go over the side? Alone?"

"Aye!" And from the pouch at her side she withdrew a small emerald. She grabbed his right hand and placed the gem in his calloused palm. "For the risk."

He frowned, clearly weighing her sanity.

"That's my family's ship, Captain. My brother's aboard." He was probably *below,* but she was striving to be succinct.

Understanding dawned on Akimba even as his frown lines deepened. "I'm sorry, Miss Raas." He sounded sincere. "There's nothing you can do."

"There's little risk, and you're being well compensated."

Akimba stared at the gem. His voice softened as he met her eyes. "I can't take this. Not in good conscience. You'd be killed."

She showed teeth in a mirthless grin. "That's my look-out, Captain."

He stared at her only a moment longer before his fingers closed over the emerald. His voice deepened as he roared an order. "Helmsman, tack us four points to starboard!"

Even as the thickset man at the wheel growled acknowledgment, Akimba was shouting orders to the men in the masts. The cluster of passengers shifted along the deck and a handful advanced toward the helm, presumably to protest at a course change that even they could see put them closer to the pirate's line.

"I've got to get my gear," Mirian said.

"Make it fast," Akimba growled.

She dashed for the port gangway, threw herself down the ladderlike stairs, and pushed through the tiny door to her cabin. Precious seconds flew as she unlocked and opened the curved lid of her sea chest.

Mirian withdrew the weathered sword belt and the sheathed cutlass that hung from it. After a moment's hesitation she pulled off her blouse, leaving her torso garbed only in a tight undershirt. She dropped the garment into the chest.

She fumbled off her sandals, then slung her sword belt over one shoulder, put the key to the lock, and bowed her head briefly. Eyes closed, she asked for blessings—from Desna, goddess of luck, and from her ancestors. For the first time, she realized the latter now included her father. "Guide my hand," she finished.

She dashed barefoot up to the weather deck. Chilton, the handsome first mate, addressed a gaggle of middle-aged colonial merchants and their families. Akimba was at the wheel, the air of immersion in his duties shielding him from the protestations below. A steady wind belled the sails and tore holes in the mist. The pirate was slowing as she neared the *Daughter*. For a moment the view was clear enough that she saw marauders readying swords along the pirate's taffrail. The numbers indeed looked daunting.

Akimba glanced at her. "Closer than I dare, Miss Raas." He looked almost apologetic. "You know my first duty is to the people and property entrusted to the *Leopard*." He continued before she could thank him. "I'm sure you have some special salvaging gear, but think: what can one person do here?"

"Never underestimate the element of surprise, Captain. You'll ship my dunnage to my mother at the Raas estate?"

"Aye, woman. You've paid me for both shipping and your suicide. May Gozreh bless you. Go!" He sounded angry, but she touched his shoulder in gratitude, for he'd brought his ship to within four cable lengths. She held off promising him a drink when next she saw him. Like most Ijo, Akimba probably had a healthy belief in sea ghosts. She didn't want to sound like she planned to haunt him.

Mirian felt the eyes of the ship's crew and passengers as she ran for the rail, and heard them speculating about the mad native woman.

She'd show them mad.

Mirian dove neatly over the side and passed seamlessly into a white-capped wave with the tiniest of splashes.

The water of Desperation Bay in the spring was only a little cool. The salt in her eyes was the worst transition, though one she'd expected. She kicked on, swimming steadily as her eyes adjusted.

Already the twin rings she wore had powered into effect. In appearance, they were virtually identical—plain black bands etched with sharp-tipped waves. Above water they seemed unre-markable. Below, they were something else entirely.

The ring on her right hand granted her the ability to move through water with the same ease she moved through air. Though she could still push against the water to swim, there was somehow no drag or delay in her actions.

More obvious were the magics activated by the ring on her left hand. The moment she'd struck the water, yellow translucent gills had blossomed along her neck. Matching flippers encased her naked calves, and glowing fins extended from her elbow to her wrist, tapering as they went.

These rare items were her heritage, one of two matched sets of arcane tools handed down from her eccentric great-grandmother. When she'd last seen the other pair, they'd been in her father's possession. She assumed they were now worn by her brother, likely somewhere underwater nearby.

Mirian surfaced to get her bearings, rising only far enough to see the *Daughter*'s hull, dead ahead.

She kicked onward, felt her curly hair streaming out to brush her shoulders. A school of silver minnows darted past, pursued by a trio of hand-sized yellow arrow fish. Far below, a sea turtle browsed in a patch of sea grass waving on the edge of the drop-off to deeper waters

She spotted the pirate's hull as it swept up beside the *Daughter*, a dark shape that blotted light. Grimly, she kicked with her full strength, willing herself to swim with all her might. Every moment she delayed might cost a life.

Agonizing minutes later she reached the pirate ship's side. There were no sharks, the gods be praised. Maybe these pirates weren't the sort who threw bloodied victims overboard.

Or maybe they just hadn't gotten started yet.

Mirian focused on the pirate's hull, looking for weakness as she kicked along. It probably lost a knot or two whenever it moved, owing to the barnacles encrusted everywhere. Yards of seaweed dangled from the keel like weird undersea banners.

Mirian opened the stiff pouch that dangled from the left side of her belt and grasped the haft of the third tool that was her family legacy. Here in the shadows, the wand was only a slim dark stick the length of her forearm. In direct sunlight it was a dull ivory banded in green. According to family record, her great-grandmother Mellient had waded into battle with a sword in one hand and her wand in the other. But Mirian Raas had little to no magical aptitude. Sometimes the wand refused to work for her, even when she gave it her full concentration. It was the most challenging of all her magical tools—and the most deadly. It was also the only one that required maintenance. After that Bandu assault outside

Kalabuto, she had only seven charges remaining in the weapon. She'd have to make every one count.

She leveled the wand and concentrated. A stream of bubbles left her mouth as she said, "Sterak."

A line of green energy streamed from the wand's tip, striking the tarred planks with an audible hiss, burning a head-sized hole through the port hull halfway between keel and waterline. The rupture sent more bubbles streaming toward the surface. The expanding edges glowed green as the acidic energy ate into the wood.

She swam on. Three more times she struck. By the last she thought the ship might truly be listing: an undeniable distraction.

Mirian swam straight on to the smaller hull of the ship she knew so well. The *Daughter* showed little sea growth, but then her father and Rendak always meticulously saw to her care. Mirian had so often navigated to the starboard ladder that she could practically reach it with her eyes closed. She hung suspended beneath it for an agonizing minute to undo the jute knot securing her hilt, hoping her delay didn't mean people were dying above. But there was no going forward until she had her sword free.

As the twine drifted, she saw a flash of movement from below the pirate ship. A distant creature swam toward her with a glowing yellow eye.

She readied the wand.

Only when she saw a second light behind the man carrying the first did she understand. She was looking at salvagers returning from the deeper water, each carrying a glowing, fist-sized stone. The man in front was a shirtless, paunchy colonial with a black fringe beard and receding hair: Rendak, the *Daughter*'s first mate and a seasoned salvager. His mouth enclosed one end of a tube that stretched over one shoulder. Mirian knew it was attached to one of the enchanted air bottles her grandfather had purchased when the salvaging team grew larger.

Rendak halted a few yards from her, his expression torn between pleasure and concern. He'd obviously noted the strange ship, as well as Mirian. Perhaps he thought she'd arrived on it. The second figure swam up beside him, his lips likewise about a tube that led to a shoulder pack—Gombe, the broad-shouldered Mulaa salvager who'd joined the team a year before Mirian left. Where was Kellic?

Explanations and a reunion would have to wait.

She pointed to the hull and gave the salvagers a hand sign that signified pirates. Rendak's eyes widened. He was a little heavier, a little grayer than she remembered, but he still looked more than capable. Bald Gombe was trim and fit.

She then pointed to the lights and brought her hands together. Rendak nodded and dimmed the glowing stone. That was new equipment. Gombe hesitated before doing the same.

Three against forty or so was better than one against forty or so . . . Mirian pushed the odds from her mind and focused her attention on the ship. She thought she heard shouts above. Hopefully that was the pirates expressing outrage at the calamity overtaking their foundering vessel.

She indicated herself and the ladder, then pointed the salvagers toward the ship's prow. Rendak gave a thumbs-up.

Mirian waited just below the surface, watching as the two men swam for the *Daughter*'s prow. Despite the irk of additional delay, she judged it best to time their attack to occur at the same moment as her own.

She breathed out while still underwater, then took a slow breath after breaching the surface. It was a hard fight not to cough. Magical assistance or no, her lungs had to acclimatize once more to air. She steadied herself with the ladder.

From the deck came the sounds of men shouting for others to stand still, the clomp of boots.

There was no telling how many pirates were really up there, or whether they'd actually been inconvenienced by her attack on their ship's hull. She might have overestimated the damage, or it might not yet have been noticed.

She supposed she'd find out. She started stealthily up the ladder, through the mist.

2

Treasures in the Deep
Ivrian

*You ask how I first met Mirian Raas? She came to me through
a miasma of fog and blood, like some avenging angel dealing
death with both hands.*

——From *The Daughter of the Mist*

At nineteen, Ivrian knew one of his mother's sales pitches
when he heard one—but then, he also detected the sound
of opportunity. With surety, Alderra Galanor meant to take him
on a salvaging expedition in hopes he'd be lured by the lucrative
opportunities that allegedly turned up when you worked for the
Sargavan government.

Nevertheless, what better chance to stock up on ideas for plays
and stories than to talk to people who'd actually had adventures?
He could hear wild tales from sailors in every dockside tavern, but
not firsthand accounts from actual salvagers—and the famed Raas
family salvagers at that.

And so he left the second act he'd been drafting in his desk
drawer and borrowed money from his mother for a sealskin pouch
to protect his papers from ocean spray. Under a pseudonym, he'd
already written a line of moderate sellers about pirate depredations.
But a serial character—a heroic salvager, say—might bring in some
real money, and then he wouldn't be beholden to Mother any longer.

The problem was that the *Daughter of the Mist* didn't seem
to *have* any heroic salvagers. Leovan Raas was dead, and his son

sent word at the last minute he would not be accompanying them. That left a fairly typical ship's crew, only two of whom were veteran salvagers, and neither of them was the sort who'd appeal to pamphlet readers.

Captain Rendak was a short, broad commoner, though the sun had burned him nearly as brown as a native. He was well muscled, but going to fat around his belly, and his hairline was receding. He'd be winning no beauty contests, nor would his first mate, a native named Gombe with ears too large for his shaved head. Worse, no one was ready or willing to chat; they were too busy with ship's duties. All Ivrian learned in four hours sailing south-west was that the crew was searching for the wreck of the *Amber Queen*, sunk a hundred and fifty years previous with a hull of gold looted from a Kalabuto ruin.

They dropped anchor a few leagues beyond Eleder Point. Alderra Galanor watched solemnly as Rendak and Gombe pulled on eelskin shoulder satchels, took up short spears, and slipped over the side.

From morning to afternoon to evening, Ivrian watched them rise near the ship's ladder, report in, and descend again. It was only when he finally got Tokello, the thickset native healer woman, talking about the Raas family and old Leovan's dives that things got interesting enough to break open his pouch and take notes.

That elder could certainly spin a tale. Take, for example, the time Leovan had discovered a ruined city ten leagues west of the Bay of Senghor, complete with chests brimming with gold, a beautiful mermaid, and a tribe of savage fish people who chased him through an underwater maze. Or the time Leovan had gambled his life for the lives of his crew against a hideous storm witch who was furious he'd drawn water from the springs on her tiny island. Even if it wasn't true, Leovan Raas was clearly the sort of man Ivrian could base stories around, a landholder who'd spurned the privilege that was his birthright for the love of adventure, surrounded by faithful friends and aided by ancient artifacts.

"How did he die?" Ivrian asked.

Tokello's smile faded. "You'll have to ask his son."

And just like that, the stories dried up. The big healer went aft to her tiny cabin, allegedly to pray.

Rendak and Gombe resurfaced a little later and climbed aboard, ordered the ship in motion, then dropped anchor a half hour west for a final dive. They'd only been down for a few minutes when the mist started to roll in. Fog was apparently an occasional navigational hazard in these waters, and the crew seemed untroubled by it.

Tokello emerged from her cabin to pace the deck, peering into the gloom, but avoided Ivrian's hopeful glances. The little boat didn't have a mast heavy enough to support a crow's nest, so sailors were posted both forward and aft as lookouts.

Ivrian returned to find his mother standing near the ladder, looking over the side. Though ever proper, Alderra Galanor was hardly dressed like the typical Sargavan noblewoman. Instead of a fine dress, her thin frame was clad only in loose breeches and a tailored short-sleeved shirt, only barely rendered fashionable by the blue cravat that matched her eyes. Her light Chelish skin was browned from a sun her peers strove studiously to avoid with parasols and wide-brimmed hats.

As she turned her head to acknowledge Ivrian, he wondered again whether the theatrical touches of black among her silver locks were entirely natural. He hoped they were. She was a handsome woman still; he'd been told he resembled her, and hoped that he would age as well.

"So," he whispered. "Why are we here, really?"

His mother's eyes flashed. "For two weeks, Kellic Raas has had this ship searching for his pet wreck, and they've turned up nothing. I thought it high time to look in on my investment."

"And they're coming up empty."

"Yes."

"The baron's hoping to salvage some money out of a wreck to pay our yearly tithe to the pirates, is that it?"

"I've been authorized," his mother said quietly, "to venture some funds to seek additional, greater revenue sources."

"So money's tight, then?"

"Yes. Money is 'tight.'" Alderra's clipped words betrayed her irritation. Ivrian knew the tone well and steeled himself for another lecture about the way the world "really" worked. "You do realize what happens if money *remains* tight, don't you?"

"Yes, Mother."

"I don't think you do. The only thing standing between Sargava and the retribution of our former masters in Cheliax is the Free Captains of the Shackles. And their fee to protect our waters gets a little steeper every year." She sighed and, fortunately, turned back to nearer matters rather than gathering steam to attack "impractical notions" about frivolous creative pursuits when real money and power was at stake. "Leo thought that the *Queen* was farther out, and spent several years searching for her." His mother glanced back at him. "Leovan Raas."

"I know."

"Kellic thinks she might have sunk a little farther in. And I think it's becoming clear that he's dead wrong."

"I'm beginning to guess why the salvagers themselves looked so unenthusiastic," Ivrian said.

"They were Leo's crew. Now that he's dead, Kellic's giving the orders, but I don't think he's got the talent." She sighed. "A pity his sister didn't stay on."

"His sister?"

"His full sister, Mirian, not the half-sister that married Lord Goleman. Mirian seems the only one of the bunch that inherited any of Leo's talent. But she wandered off years ago."

"Mirian," Ivrian repeated. Why was that name familiar? "Why'd she go?"

His mother eyed him sharply. "I gather she wasn't interested in taking over the family business."

Ivrian could relate to that.

Clearly his mother knew it, because she started in. "I'd hoped you'd see some leadership in action today. If we ever come out with them again, I think I'll bring some salvaging gear of our own so we can see to the work below as well."

Ivrian barely heard her, because he had been seized by a new idea. "What's Mirian like?"

"She was always sharp-eyed—like her father. Quick-witted. And I hear she was a natural in the water."

"What did she look like?"

"I haven't seen her for years. She was a gangly thing. Darker than Kellic. Pretty. She took after her mother."

Ivrian was far more interested in handsome men than pretty women, but he knew a good thing when he heard it. This daughter of a famous salvager could be the star of his stories—a proud Sargavan woman fighting to keep her country free from the devil-sworn puppets of the Chelish Empire. He could envision a dark adventuress on the cover of the first leaflet now. And she'd be drawn with generous cleavage, of course. Even if some colonials would turn up their noses at the idea of a half-native heroine, that should still attract some interest.

"Sail to stern!" the lookout cried. And then: "She's bearing down fast. Gozreh preserve us, she's raised the black flag!"

The crew scurried like ants, but with neither captain nor mate aboard, no one seemed to know what to do.

Alderra turned from the rail, voice crisp and commanding. "Sailors! Panic gets you nowhere! You two—bring out the weapons!"

Though the commands came from an unexpected quarter, they were quickly obeyed. The crew seemed grateful to have someone providing direction. A pair of sailors ran down the gangway. The remaining dozen watched the oncoming ship.

"Pirates?" Ivrian asked his mother. "What are they doing in these waters? They're not supposed to attack us!" By terms of Sargava's agreement with the Free Captains, any ship flying the Sargavan flag was to remain unmolested. He checked—sure enough, the white flag of Sargava with its single black square and vertical red line flapped beneath the little blue family pennant. No one could have missed it.

"You may have to explain that to them," Alderra said.

He ignored her sarcasm. "Can't we sail away?"

"There's no time. They'll be on us before we could raise canvas."

The two sailors sent belowdecks clambered back with a heavy chest. They set it down just beyond the gangway and threw it open. Inside was the gleam of metal, and the sailors filed forward to lift cutlasses even as the prow of the pirate ship neared the *Daughter*'s stern. The mist parted long enough for Ivrian to see dozens upon dozens of snarling faces lined along the railing, ten or twelve feet higher than their own.

Tokello had appeared out of nowhere and approached Alderra directly. "Lady Galanor, our crew can't take them on. You'll get all of us killed."

One large, black-haired pirate called loudly to lay down their arms if they wanted to live.

Tokello exchanged a grim look with Alderra, who had a hand on the hilt of her cutlass. For the first time, Ivrian noted that the sword was the one part of his mother's outfit that didn't look gleaming new.

She eyed the pirate, then the healer, and her frown deepened. "Down weapons," she called to the sailors, then cursed under her breath.

"There's little of value here," Ivrian whispered, gulping. "Won't they just see that and depart?"

"We can hope," his mother said grimly.

The pirate ship was a huge two-master. As it ground to a halt against their side, its deck looming above their own, Ivrian saw men with arrows nocked and a contingent with raised spears. The rest all but bristled with cutlasses.

His mother cupped her hands around her mouth. "We're no fight for you, but have little worth your trouble!"

"That's for us to decide!" a gruff voice called back.

Grappling hooks dropped to catch in the rail. Pirates swung down on ratlines. Before long, tens of them swarmed the ship, carting away food, drink, ship's supplies, and the rather sad-looking coin purses carried by the *Daughter*'s common sailors, who they'd herded together at the prow.

The chief collector was a big bronzed Keleshite with vivid blue eyes. He would have been handsome if he hadn't had such a scowl, as though he found this whole pirate business an annoyance. He didn't smile until he caught sight of Ivrian and his mother. For a moment, Ivrian thought he could flirt a little to improve their odds of survival.

"Where's your money?" The Keleshite stopped in front of them, sword leveled. "I know you're hiding jewels someplace."

The pirate had recognized them as aristocrats. His smile, Ivrian realized, was one of satisfaction, not appreciation.

While Ivrian and his mother turned out their pockets, a short, pale man with an absurdly well-groomed mustache climbed down from the high deck of the pirate ship. His eyes settled on the seal-skin pouch that Ivrian clutched.

"Take that, Mylit," he ordered the Keleshite.

The big man smiled mirthlessly at Ivrian and waggled his fingers.

"These are my writings," Ivrian said. "Of no value to anyone but me."

Mylit grabbed the bag with one hand and smashed Ivrian across the cheek with the other. The lightning attack dropped Ivrian to the planks. He blinked in pain, staring stunned at his mother's polished boots, then looked up as the little man stepped closer. Ivrian supposed *he* was the captain.

"Open it," the captain commanded. Was he Chelish? That was no colonial accent.

Ivrian blinked as he propped himself up on an elbow. His cheek stung, and he was flooded with shame, unsure if he should rise. A trio of pirates by the wheel chuckled at him. Ivrian climbed carefully to one knee, watching Mylit lift a page from the pouch. He considered it carefully, as though reading were a labor. "It's just a bunch of letters."

The captain snatched the paper, eyes roving quickly before he relaxed. Ivrian glanced longingly at the now-guarded chest of swords.

"I'm making notes for a story," he explained.

The little captain sniffed, crumpled the paper into a ball, and pitched it over the side.

Ivrian felt his eyes widen in astonishment, although words failed him.

"And where are the salvagers?" the man asked Ivrian's mother.

Alderra answered the question calmly. "My apologies, Captain, but they're diving right now."

The captain pointed a beringed finger. "You're Lady Galanor, aren't you? One of the baron's lapdogs."

"That *is* my name," Alderra said with great dignity. "You, sir, however, have me at a loss."

The captain sneered. "No, I have you at my mercy."

Mylit's laugh was interrupted by a shout from the pirate ship.

"Cap'n! We're taking on water!"

The Keleshite and the little man both whipped around. "What? How?" Mylit demanded.

The deck lurched, and Ivrian fought for footing. The pirate ship had listed, and as it creaked to starboard the grappling ropes tightened and tilted the *Daughter* to port.

The Keleshite shouted for his crew to get back across and get to the pumps. Most of the boarding party scrambled over. Now it seemed to Ivrian as though Mylit commanded the crew. Who, then, was the fellow with the mustache?

The mustached little man pointed accusingly at Alderra. "This is the work of your salvagers, isn't it? They're attacking the ship?"

"I don't know how they could," Alderra said reasonably. "They're only armed with spears."

"You're lying. Mylit, just kill her," he fumed.

The Keleshite pulled a cutlass from his belt. As he lifted it, an emerald beam of energy shot out from behind Ivrian engulfed the pirate's arm. The huge man screamed, and his sword clattered to the deck as cloth and flesh dissolved in bubbling smoke.

Ivrian hesitated no longer. He snatched the cutlass as it came to rest, still ringing from its fall. He lunged at Mylit even as a second blast caught the mustachioed man in the shoulder. Ivrian stabbed the pirate straight through the chest, turning his scream to a ragged gurgle. The man dropped and breathed his last.

Ivrian hadn't ever attacked someone outside of a practice bout before, and if he'd had time to reflect, he might have been appalled. Caught up in the moment, however, he advanced with a flourish and a shout, as though he were on the stage. The nearest pirates backed off. His rush was enough of a distraction for his mother to draw her own blade, and for three of the *Daughter*'s sailors to rush the weapons chest.

But the pirates were not easily cowed. Ivrian caught a swing on the late Mylit's notched blade, a little higher than he'd hoped. While he tried to untangle from his foe, he had to lean left to miss a beheading from a different snarling pirate.

Suddenly his mother was beside him, wielding her cutlass with astonishing vigor. The onslaught enabled Ivrian to break free and plunge his sword through an enemy's throat.

"Less flash, son," his mother said, as if coaching the proper use of a salad fork at a state dinner.

The fight was furious. He was vaguely aware there remained at least one pirate for every member of the *Daughter*'s crew, but he had to focus on the hairy face above the gnarled, sword-wielding hands that thrust and sliced right at him. He chopped one deadly edge away, leapt a stab from an evil-looking Halfling he hadn't noticed earlier, then cut through the little man's head.

He dispatched the other pirate, who had turned to grab a nearby line back to his own ship, then took stock of the area around him. He saw three foes rushing Tokello, apparently eager for easy prey, and he stepped in her direction, but she raised her arms and called out for Gozreh to protect her. After that, none of the men could close on her, and Ivrian guessed she'd worked some spell.

She might have been safe, but that meant all three turned their attention to Ivrian. They grinned as they spread out to flank him.

A dripping-wet woman suddenly leapt to his side, her cutlass sweeping to clear space and stopping the pirates in their tracks. Even as Ivrian was wondering who in Shelyn's name *she* was, Tokello shouted, "Mirian!" with the sort of conviction usually reserved for declaring thanks to deities.

This was Mirian Raas? Ivrian stared. Where had she come from?

While her brother was light enough to look almost full-blood colonial, Mirian clearly took after her native mother, as Alderra had said, with rich dark skin and a dripping mass of black hair.

She also looked dangerous and capable, rippling with sleek muscles under her clinging, sodden clothes. She leaned away from a one-eyed pirate's clumsy overhand slash and cut deep into his arm. While the fellow screamed, she kicked him off balance into a second foe, then followed with a thrust that skewered both. The third pirate turned to run. She leapt after and hacked him down, then dashed on without a backward glance.

"Boy!" Tokello cried. "Cut that line!" She pointed to a grappling hook buried in the *Daughter*'s straining starboard rail.

Ivrian parted the tense rope easily. Captain Rendak had appeared from nowhere, also dripping wet, and was bellowing at his men to free the sails.

Someone on the pirate ship sent an arrow thudding into the planks a hand-span from Ivrian's boot, and an arrow pierced a sailor on his left.

He glanced up and around.

Mirian downed her final opponent with a powerful slice, then turned and raised a wand, shouting an arcane word as she did so. A line of green energy blasted from the end of the weapon and felled an archer wedged along the tilted and now significantly lowered pirate deck. He slid out of sight with a scream, his bow clattering after him. Others were clambering to take his place, but Gombe and Lady Galanor warded them off with well-cast spears. Ivrian worried that the pirates planned to drop to the *Daughter*'s deck.

Mirian pointed her sword at Ivrian. For a moment he thought she might attack him. "You, cut the rutting anchor!"

He knew right where it was, over near the ladder. He split the thick old rope with two good swings.

The main canvases dropped, and sailors slid down the braces to secure the sheets even as Rendak flung himself at the wheel. The wind caught the caravel and the *Daughter* swayed away from the pirate ship even as a final spray of arrows rained down. All but one missed: Ivrian saw it strike Rendak's arm.

The older man cursed and kept a hand to the wheel, no matter the shaft and point protruding through one large biceps.

It was only then that Ivrian felt a little green. Perhaps it was the blood dripping from Rendak's wound, or the blood on his own sword, or all the bodies, or that he'd suddenly realized how many times he'd come close to death in the last few minutes. The gentlemanly sword schools his mother had sent him to and the showy moves he'd learned working with actors really hadn't prepared him for the *result* of bladework.

He sat down beside the rail, his face cool and moist, and concentrated on not throwing up. With measured care, he turned his head, for it seemed any sudden movement might make him ill. The stranded pirate ship showed no signs of following. For some reason, its deck was canted at almost thirty degrees.

The *Daughter of the Mist* tacked away, catching nearly the full strength of the wind as she turned north by northwest— or at least, that's what the sailors called to one another. Dead pirates were tossed over the side, though he noticed Mirian Raas and his mother searching both the man with the mustache and Mylit.

The two women were doing quite a lot of talking. Ivrian rather wished he felt well enough to listen in. He tried to rise, but grew dizzy and sat back down.

He watched Tokello walk among the crew. Two of the *Daughter's* sailors were apparently done for, but a fellow in a striped shirt who'd been holding his chest was now talking with a mate as he was helped belowdecks.

Tokello tended five others for minor wounds before coming finally to Rendak. He turned the bridge over to Gombe and faced Tokello, offering his wounded arm.

Mirian and Ivrian's mother, still in conversation, stepped into the cabin at the back of the quarterdeck. Ivrian stood up to follow, but then Tokello cut the arrowhead with her huge knife and pulled the shaft out of Rendak's arm by the black fletching.

That final spurt of blood from Rendak's wound was the push that brought Ivrian to the rail's edge, where he vomited lunch and breakfast out onto the churning waves.

3

Percentages and Proofs
Mirian

Mirian frowned as she took in the shambles the pirates had left of the narrow captain's cabin. Fading light from the slim galley windows spilled over broken desk drawers and torn papers and charts scattered across the deck. The mattress from the bunk under the windows had been slashed apart, probably in a search for hidden valuables.

At least the little dining table was intact, although one of its chairs lay with a smashed back—the one at the head of the table, where her father would have sat. Fitting.

One of the few unsullied items was the wood carving Mirian laid carefully on the table. She'd found it tossed aside on the deck above, dropped in the mad scramble before the bloodshed. Her mother's work, in brown and blond woods, showing Leovan smiling, with Mirian herself grinning up at him. How old had she been? Nine? Eleven? Her fingers trembled as she returned the carving to the nail that had secured it to the bulkhead, but the bracket on the carving's back was warped, and it wouldn't hang straight. She thought she might be able to fix that, at least. Her eyes dropped to her fingers, trying to decide if they shook with anger or sorrow.

She heard the light step of Lady Galanor behind her and the click of the cabin door as the noblewoman shut it.

"Please, sit, m'lady." Mirian forced calm into her voice. "I apologize for the décor."

"I'm sorry for it as well," the woman replied as she righted a chair to settle on.

Mirian rooted among the shirts lying beside a chest that had been hacked open. Rendak's clothes, not her father's. With a muttered apology she turned to remove her wet undergarment and slipped the shirt on in its place. Rendak's arms were longer than hers, so she rolled the sleeves up to the elbow.

Mirian picked up the broken chair, then took the seat across from Lady Galanor. She rubbed at a spot on her pants she suspected was blood.

Lady Galanor wistfully contemplated the crooked carving. Here, in the dim light from the galley windows, she seemed younger.

Like many Sargavan nobles, Lady Galanor was olive-skinned, with a proud hawk's beak of a nose. Her shoulders were high with assurance. Yet she lacked some of the arrogance of manner so common to aristocrats, and judging from her skillful swordplay, she was no layabout. Mirian gave up trying to guess her age. Was she prematurely silver, or simply an older woman who'd stayed in shape?

Lady Galanor smiled apologetically. "Thank you, again, Miss Raas."

"Thank Desna," Mirian demurred. "I happened along at the right time."

"I shall praise her for your timing, and you for everything else." A glance back at the carving. "There was a spark in you when you were a child. I see it has flared into something grand."

Mirian looked more closely at the woman, but couldn't recall seeing her before. "You knew me as a child?"

Lady Galanor smiled wistfully. "Your father and I were close friends once. I helped him found the Sargavan Adventurer's Club."

"The club?" She eyed the woman across from her even more carefully. Father and a small band of like-minded Sargavans had purchased a building where they could celebrate their exploits, trade information, and, naturally, drink. The club's failure had been a bitter memory for him.

"It was a fine notion," Lady Galanor said. "But like many fine notions in Sargava, it was crushed under the weight of tradition."

Mirian considered Lady Galanor's face and tried to subtract the years. She was still striking now; what would she have looked like twenty or thirty years ago? Was she looking at one of her father's former lovers? "Father never mentioned you."

Lady Galanor's smile turned sad. "I'm employed by the baron, the Noble Custodian of Sargava. I've had to be away for long periods. Your father and I hadn't seen much of each other for a long time."

And how much of each other did you see before that? Mirian had decided to humor Lady Galanor's request for a private chat, but there were things that needed doing, the least of which was fixing this cabin. She wanted to look in on Rendak, find out why the *Daughter* was here, and learn why her brother wasn't aboard. It was time to speed things along. "You said you wanted to talk to me about something important."

The aristocrat reached into a pocket and produced the rumpled letters she'd taken off the pirate's leader. "The captain was commanded by that Chelish man."

So she'd said outside. Why couldn't they discuss this on the deck? Mirian nodded.

Lady Galanor touched the paper. "Someone without a signature specifically ordered him to target your ship. And me."

"It's not *my* ship," Mirian said. "But go on. Why were they after you?"

Lady Galanor folded her hands and cleared her throat. "I'm raising funds for the yearly tithe. And the Chelaxians want to stop that, naturally. Before he died, your father was setting up a salvaging expedition into the interior he thought would be particularly helpful to our cause. Did he mention anything about it to you?"

Mirian shook off a shiver. She wasn't getting any warmer as the sun went down. "I haven't heard from my father since I left home six years ago. My mother wrote once a month, but the messages didn't always reach me right away. I only learned of his death last week."

"I see. I'm sorry for your loss, then."

"We were no longer close." Mirian's fingers found a loose thread in Rendak's shirt to pull. She thought of the man her father used to be. "Lady Galanor, my father was perhaps the least prejudiced colonial ever born, with one exception—he despised Sargavan nobles. Passionately. If you let him, he could rant about them for hours. It's not that I doubt your story, it's—"

"Of course he hated them. It was Lady Daugustana who drove the wedge between Leo and his first wife." Lady Galanor tapped the table near the carving for emphasis. "And it was Lady Daugustana and her cronies who destroyed the club. We wanted to move Sargava forward, and the old always want to keep it the same." She laughed. "Now I'm the old."

"Not as old as Daugustana."

"Hah. No, not nearly. Mirian—may I call you Mirian? I did, once, when you were very young."

"You may," Mirian said cautiously. "Pardon me, m'lady. I wouldn't mind a little light, would you?"

"You may call me Alderra. And yes, that would be appreciated."

Both lanterns hung above the table had somehow escaped the wrath of the pirates. After rooting around through one of the cracked drawers lying on the deck, Mirian located flint, steel, and a length of slow-burn cable. In a moment her practiced hands had lit the lanterns, obligingly opened by Alderra.

Once flames were flickering in the glass, Mirian blew out the cable and returned it to the drawer. As she bent to set the drawer into the desk beside the door she caught sight of a familiar panel in the bulkhead at knee level.

Why not? She pressed her palm to the wood. Concealed behind the ordinary plank was a narrow cubby where her father usually kept a bottle of wine. There was still a bottle there, although as she lifted it to the light, she found it a dark amber rather than the red she expected.

Leovan Raas's tastes had apparently changed over the years. Or Rendak had found the wine cache and replaced it with something he liked better.

"A drink, Alderra?" Mirian said. "I can't vouch for the vintage, and I'm not sure I have any glasses. I believe its whiskey."

"After that scrape, I can't say I'm picky."

Mirian uncorked the bottle, sniffed, and passed it to her.

Alderra took a swig and seemed satisfied. "Heady stuff." She handed it back.

The aristocrat was right. The whiskey opened with a kick and closed with a smooth fade. Mirian held it up to the lantern light but couldn't make out the writing on the label.

Lady Galanor cleared her throat. "Here's my problem, Miss Raas. Your father died as he was finishing up a dive on an unrelated venture. I allowed some weeks to pass before I pursued the matter with your brother, and that is perhaps where I erred." She smiled glumly. "I did not wish to push business matters during a mourning period."

Lady Galanor seemed to want some sort of response. "Understandable," Mirian said.

"By the time I asked your brother about the expedition your father planned, he told me he had dismissed the other parties involved."

"Other parties?" Mirian was still thinking about her father's death. Her mother's account had been vague.

"Lizardfolk. Kellic said he found them 'unseemly.'"

"Unseemly," Mirian repeated. That didn't sound like the Kellic she knew, a boy who'd followed Father like a puppy, imitating his every gesture.

"I've decided to hire *you* to find the lizardfolk that your father planned to work with. And then lead the salvage team."

Mirian plunked the bottle down unintentionally hard—a ringing thunk filled the little cabin. "Alderra, I didn't come back to run the business. I returned to comfort my mother and throw some flowers on my father's grave. I intend to depart Eleder and its embalmed grandeur at the earliest opportunity."

Alderra Galanor contemplated her before gesturing for the bottle and pulling another swig. "There are good people in Eleder. They need your help."

"I'm a Pathfinder now, m'lady. Alderra," she corrected herself. "I left my team at a dig site north of Freehold. They need me there."

"Do they? What if Eleder needs you more?"

"Eleder needs a half-native salvager? Tell me another."

Alderra smiled thinly. "The baron knows Sargava needs to move forward. He's hampered by crones like Daugustana and all the petty councilors. He has to fight for every tiny concession. Extending that road down through the city outskirts—"

"The slums?"

"If you like."

"They're slums."

"The baron extended the main road through the slums last year so the laborers wouldn't be calf-deep in mud during rainy season. To get enough votes to put it through the house, he had to promise a tax break to the nobles for the next three years. And that's put him in a bind, because there's one large payment that has to be made every year unless we want a Chelish fleet at our quays."

"To the Free Captains."

"Yes. Daugustana and her ilk won't find their money much use if Cheliax sails back in and reclaims our country, but they're blind to the threat. They're obsessed with their little games, conveniently forgetting that without the pirate fleet protecting our waters, they'd all be kicking from a gibbet, or screaming on the tines."

"Eleder's petty politics, Lady Galanor, are just part of the reason I left."

"So I gather." Alderra paused but didn't follow up that line of thought. "I must find a revenue source so we can pay our tithe to the Free Captains of the Shackles. Your brother has been wasting my time poking around the deeps for a wreck ever since your father died, and produced nothing. I cannot continue working with your family unless you take over."

"That's unfortunate," Mirian said. "But I'm not interested."

Alderra's eyebrows lowered. "If you find me the lizardfolk and set up the salvage run, I'll cut the Raas family in for twenty percent of the profit."

Mirian blinked away her astonishment. "Let me get this straight: You mean to induce me by taking *eighty percent*? While I find the salvage drop, furnish the ship and the experts, and run the risk? Why should I give you any percent at all?"

Alderra cleared her throat. "It's possible that you're not aware of certain circumstances." She watched Mirian for a reaction.

"What circumstances?"

"This is awkward." Alderra took a deep breath, observing Mirian, as though she expected her to interrupt at any moment. "Your family is heavily in debt. There's little room left to meet those obligations apart from selling off your ship or your home. Perhaps both will be needed."

Mirian stared, seeking meaning in words that made no sense. She searched the older woman's face for some sign that this was a joke. One in terrible taste. Could Alderra be telling the truth? Where would her family live without the house? Mother and Kellic would be devastated, to say nothing of the men and women who worked for them both in the home and on the ship. How would they make a living?

Alderra's expression softened. "I'm sorry. I see now that you had no idea."

"No," Mirian managed, finally. She felt flushed. It'd been a long while since she'd downed such potent whiskey. She was surprised by how calm she sounded. "Is this your doing? Is that how you maneuvered my father into working for you?"

"What? No! I had nothing to do with your father's choices, my dear. I gather he's had a hard time of it for the last few years. I needed his help, and I thought he could use mine."

Mirian felt that flush fading. Lady Galanor could be lying, but it was more likely her father had run into some bad luck. Salvaging had its lean years. And it would be just like Mother not to send word of anything upsetting. It was a wonder she'd even written to inform her about her father's death. "How did he get into so much debt?"

"He sank a great deal of money into a new ship, and there was a dockyard fire when it was two-thirds built. Apparently he promised more than he actually had to spend."

Father had occasionally dreamed about a larger ship, but Mirian had never thought he'd actually want to part with the *Daughter*.

Alderra misread her silence as skepticism. "I'm not trying to threaten you, Mirian. That twenty percent should be enough to pay off the debts and leave you with a little profit as well."

Mirian set the bottle back down and found herself asking: "Twenty percent of how much?"

"Did you ever play cards with your father? He kept things very close to his chest. All I know is that he promised a fortune in gems. Enough to drown the crone."

The crone being Lady Daugustana. Mirian felt a smile pull at the corner of her mouth. "Now *that* sounds like my father. But he was prone to exaggerate."

"When he told a tale, yes. But not when he gave his word. Leo shook hands on it with me, Mirian. I believed him. And I believe in you. You can find the necessary partners and lead the salvage team."

It was strange to hear this woman calling Father by his first name, and in such a comfortable way. Again she wondered just how close Alderra and her father had once been.

Mirian ran her eyes along the carved image of her father's face tilting heavenward on the wall. "I'm not as skilled at salvaging. Not like he was at his prime."

"Perhaps not. But he wasn't in his prime when we shook on it."

That was surely true. Long years had passed since her father was that smiling, bronzed man who could shrug off whatever the world threw his way. In the years before Mirian left, the bitterness had worn him down, and more and more often those powerful shoulders had been fortified by a constant influx of alcohol.

She thought about the trio of Pathfinders waiting for her in Freehold. Tyrin was seasoned enough to manage things until she got back. She frowned, remembering that mosaic they'd found the day before she left. She'd dearly wanted to make a good sketch of it, but Tyrin could probably handle that duty as well. She'd have to write him with instructions.

For now, it looked as though she would be stuck here. "All right, then."

"There's one more thing you need to know: the Chelish may have played a part in your father's death."

"How do you know?"

"I don't. Not for sure. But they certainly appear to have tried to arrange mine. I suspect that either someone close to the baron is a Chelish spy, or . . ." she let her voice trail off. "I'm afraid I shall have to be indelicate. Your brother has taken up with a Chelish woman."

Mirian's voice cracked like a whip. "You're implying my brother was involved in my father's death?"

"I didn't say that. Spies can be very clever. They can sew information together from little threads. If she is a spy, and Kellic happened to mention where your father was diving, it would be all she needed to act. Without him, the arrangement fell through, which is awfully convenient for Chelish interests, don't you think?"

Mirian fingered the neck of the bottle and let out a low sigh. She dearly wanted another drink, but decided against it. She was near her limit.

"I know it's a lot to take in all at once. And, in all fairness, your brother's paramour may be completely innocent."

"Suppose," Mirian said, "my brother's the only one who knows where to find the lizardfolk? If I have to talk to him about it, he might talk to this woman."

"You'll have to ask him not to do that."

She hadn't seen Kellic in years. She didn't relish the idea of casually working "your lover might be a Chelish spy" into the conversation.

"I didn't promise that your job would be simple," Alderra reminded her.

"Nothing good is ever simple." Mirian tapped the table a last time, then thrust her hand across it. "Very well, Alderra. It seems I've little choice."

The noblewoman shook her hand formally. "You had other choices. They just weren't good ones."

4

Reunion
Mirian

By the time Mirian joined Rendak at the prow she could see the stone walls of Eleder rising along the darkening coast. The fog had rolled away with the evening breeze, leaving a clear view of the city from leagues away. It sprawled beyond its great walls. Distant lights twinkled a white-and-golden welcome, although Mirian knew most were lanterns hung in harbor taverns, gambling halls, and brothels in the deliberate buffer zone between the wharf and the proper city districts. The city had to be open to the Free Captains, but the governing elders preferred to trap them in a single district, where there would be plenty to distract them from advancing into more upscale neighborhoods.

Mirian had already asked about Rendak's arm, which he'd reported as sore but healing, and his family, which he reported as fair. And then she began to test the truth of what Alderra Galanor had told her. Right away Rendak took exception to the idea that the Chelish had anything to do with her father's death.

"Oh, no, lass." Rendak's gravelly voice fell to a low rumble. "That was sea devils. And they don't work with nobody."

Sea devil was the name all the folk of Desperation Bay gave the sharklike humanoids that laired in the deep waters and sometimes prowled the wreck of the Chelish fleet, the ships that had been sunk during Sargava's battle for independence. "Sea devils killed him?" She had a hard time believing it. "Why were you anywhere near them?"

"Money's been a little low."

"I've heard it's worse than that."

Rendak scratched the back of his neck. "Your mother tell you?"

"Lady Galanor filled me in. Are the coffers as empty as she said?"

"Empty enough to make us dive the Chelish fleet wreck. We'd had our eye on a big old four-master for years but didn't want to risk it. We figured we didn't have a choice."

"You're certain it was sea devils that killed him?"

"It was sharks that killed him," Rendak said, "but sea devils made them. We could see one of them floatin' nearby. You know how they get on with sharks. A big one sneaked up on Leo." He paused, as if to gather strength for the rest of the story, then remained silent.

"Go on." Strange. She thought she'd made peace with her father's death, and now she felt a tightening in her chest.

Rendak stared a moment, then blurted out, "He was going for the sea devil, just raising his wand at that figure floatin' out there in the dark, when the shark came out of a hole in the hull and took most of his arm off. We managed to get him away, but he'd bled out by the time we got him to Tokello."

Mirian could picture the moment too well, a mad flurry of shapes in black waters, sharks driven to frenzy by the blood. Rendak and Gombe fighting desperately with their diving spears to drive off the great predators, Gombe pulling her paling father up as Rendak swam guard.

Rendak's jaw tightened and he lowered his head. He let out a long breath, looked at her as if he wished to say more but had forgotten the words.

Mirian gripped his shoulder. "I know you did all you could, and more than you should have."

"I never thought it'd be him to go down," Rendak said.

Maybe her father's death really had been an unconnected tragedy. It didn't change that he was gone, or the state of affairs he'd left things in. "Lady Galanor said Father had lined up another salvage run that was potentially lucrative. Why didn't you hold out for that instead of risking anything near sea devil territory?"

Rendak's eyes narrowed in thought, and he dropped his voice. "You mean with the lizardfolk?"

"Aye."

"Leo said that one was likely to be dangerous, lass. More dangerous than going into the fleet wrecks. Leo was hoping we could maybe score big with a quick drop, and then we wouldn't have to go through with it."

"Did he tell you where the lizardfolk drop was?"

"No."

"What about the lizardfolk? Do you know where they went?"

Rendak shook his head.

"That's too bad. Because I'm going to have to find them."

He looked at her sidelong. "Is that what you've been talking to Lady Galanor about?"

"Yes."

A smile pulled up one corner of his beard. "You taking over?"

"Yes."

"Then you can count me in. Probably all of us." His smile broadened. "Will you be leading from here on out?"

"No. I'll help with the debt, then I'm gone."

"Huh." Rendak sounded disappointed

"Don't say a thing to anyone else. Lady Galanor thinks someone's leaking word of our plans. They were sent to sink the *Daughter* on this salvage run."

"You think someone on board's a traitor?" Rendak's eyebrows rose in astonishment.

She shook her head. "No, I think someone talked too much." She studied her father's trusted friend and hoped that she'd judged right by sharing the information with him.

Mirian shook off that moment of doubt. If she couldn't trust the loyalty of Filian Rendak, then she might as well give up on the human race. "How do you like being captain?"

Rendak grunted. "I always figured you'd be captain, once Leo was done with it."

"What about Kellic?"

Rendak scratched his neck, looked away, sighed. "He's not a salvager. He's known it for years. You were the one. That's why Leo gave you the rings. And that's why he knew you were coming back."

"Father actually said that?"

"Aye."

Mirian was a little surprised her father mentioned her at all, especially after their final conversation. She'd assumed that Leovan Raas, champion grudge-holder, would keep a closed mouth about his second daughter, just like he did his first wife, his first daughter, and the old explorer's club—anything that hadn't worked out for him, really. "What did he say?"

"That the sea was in your blood." Rendak's bold cadence briefly mimicked her father's. "That you would've turned those rings over to your brother if you meant to leave the trade forever."

"It wasn't the trade I hated, Rendak. It was Eleder."

"Oh, there are worse cities. It's what you make of it."

She couldn't keep the bitterness from her voice. "Eleder's fine, so long as you know your place."

"Leo made his place," Rendak said with pride.

"That was his problem."

"No. That was what everyone else's problem was. You want to know why Kellic doesn't salvage?" He eyed her squarely. "He wants all the little colonial lords to approve of him."

Mirian winced. "That'll never happen." The little fool. "He should know that."

"Aye."

"There are countless places across the world where they'd accept him just as he is. Even Cheliax could give a toss about the color of his skin. It only matters here."

"Things are getting better," Rendak said.

"You're just saying that because you want me to stay."

"No, really, they are. The new generation's a little more accepting."

"Then why is Kellic having trouble?"

"I didn't say things were perfect."

She snorted. "That's your sales pitch for keeping me here?"

"Give me time. I'll think of something better."

Rendak's loyalty was touching. "How's my mother?"

"You can see how Leo's death got to her, but only if you know her well. Poor thing hides behind that Bas'o pride. Stiff neck, show no emotion. You know. Sort of that look you were just giving me."

Mirian felt a grin pull weakly at her. She knew exactly what Rendak meant. Her mother had worn that same expression after any disappointment, most memorably that evening Mirian had talked a six-year-old Kellic into sneaking down to the docks with her to spy on pirates.

"That's Leo's smile! The only time you look like him, gods be praised. But you've got his spirit. You were born for this, Mirian."

"That's kind of you to say."

Rendak clapped her on the back. "Well, however long you're staying, it's sure good to see you." He swaggered off.

Mirian remained at the prow while the *Daughter* sailed on toward Eleder. It was too dark to pick out the color of the flags flown from the tall ships anchored along the long stone quays of the great harbor, but she knew that they came from all across the region, some probably from as far away as the Inner Sea.

Gombe guided them for home, along the coastline south of the city. Walled mansions stood on the low ridge above smaller wharves, each owned by the descendants of wealthy Chelish colonists who'd built beyond the protection of the central settlement. Eleder had expanded over the intervening centuries so that the mansions had been transformed from an independent community into a suburb.

Small pleasure yachts were anchored beside the dark quays of neighbors nearest the Raas dock. If things remained as they had been, the Raas's were the only ridge family that worked for a living, one of any number of strikes against them. It was perfectly fine to own ships, but colonial aristocrats certainly didn't captain them, and they didn't marry native women and father half-native children and demand they be accepted into society.

Not that there weren't thousands of half-native citizens running about Sargava. But for an aristocrat to admit having a child with a native was simply a bridge too far. Such children were acknowledged with a quiet stipend so that they could learn a trade, if at all. Only an occasional madman like her father insisted someone of mixed race be fully accepted into Sargavan high society.

Even with his straight hair and lighter skin, Mirian's younger brother Kellic had a difficult time of it, though his challenges were nothing like Mirian's. She had been treated like a servant by her peers at a series of young ladies' academies. Her last aristocratic schooling had ended in one cataclysmic moment, when her father dropped by at lunch to find her sequestered with the help. The sharp words he'd exchanged with the woman in charge would have resulted in a duel if Madame Corlander's husband had not been rightfully afraid of Leovan Raas.

Leovan always had been much better at making enemies than friends. Back then, Mirian had been embarrassed by him. Once she'd been old enough to salvage, she'd grown to idolize him. In the end, she'd realized her father was a man of complexities. He might truly believe in a colorblind society, but he also burned with deep-seated anger. As Mirian matured, she'd sometimes wondered if her father had chosen to marry a Bas'o woman in part because he knew how badly it would piss off his neighbors.

Two lanterns blazed high and bright on poles raised at the dock's end. Rendak, at the wheel himself now, guided the *Daughter* in. The usual crowd of relatives emerged from the gabled dock house and took hold of ropes tossed from the prow as they called out to their loved ones.

Some of them, she reflected grimly, would not be answering.

The moment two sailors lifted the gangplank into place, a tall figure in dress pants and a waistcoat hurried across, carrying a cane. Mirian thought at first he was one of Lady Galanor's contacts, for he moved immediately toward her and her son and offered a formal bow.

Then she heard his voice. "Lady Galanor, I hope your voyage was a pleasant one?"

Kellic. That was *Kellic*?

Rendak, meanwhile, was overseeing the ship's tying off even as some of the sailors were calling up to the huddle of waiting relatives about what had happened. The resultant gasps and lone wail drowned out Lady Galanor's response.

Mirian carefully walked around the laboring sailors, looking at her brother as she drew closer.

Tall, slim, elegantly dressed. His straight hair was pushed back from his forehead and lightly powdered, as had been the fashion in Cheliax at some point. He'd grown into a handsome man, with high broad shoulders and a gently cleft chin he'd inherited from Father. His fine nose came from Mother, though it was hard to see much of her in him without close scrutiny, for his skin appeared even lighter than Mirian remembered. Was he wearing *makeup*?

And resemblance to either parent ended completely with Kellic's wardrobe, tailored from the most expensive cloth, with more conservative lines than Leovan Raas had ever worn, complete with a brown cravat, a silver-tipped ornamental cane, and a hand that glittered with rings.

Next to him, Lady Galanor looked like a laborer.

Her brother's face fell as Lady Galanor spoke to him. Mirian drew up near Ivrian, waiting by his mother's side.

The younger Galanor offered a hopeful smile. Mirian still wasn't sure what to make of him. Ivrian's own clothing was flamboyant, and he carried himself with a sort of careless exuberance. Yet she knew he'd been a crucial player in driving back the pirates, so she nodded a bow.

Ivrian brightened and returned the gesture.

"Mirian?" Kellic had finally noticed her. "What are you— How—"

"Your sister happened to be in the right place at the right time," Lady Galanor said. "If she hadn't dived off her passenger ship to help us, the pirates would probably be sailing the *Daughter* off to Smuggler's Shiv right now. And I don't care to think what they would have done with us."

"Mirian." Kellic's eyes brightened for a moment. He grimaced at her clothing, yet nevertheless opened his arms to her. The two embraced.

They pulled apart. "What are you doing here?" he asked.

"Mother wrote me about father's death. I returned as soon as I could."

"It seems like your arrival was timely." His smile was polite. He turned back to Lady Galanor. "I'm very sorry to hear that you were placed in danger, Lady Galanor." His eyes slipped over to where shrouded forms were being carried up the gangplank. "Gods."

"We lost some crew," Mirian said.

"That's terrible," he said. "Terrible news. I don't suppose Rendak found anything to make all of this worthwhile?"

Mirian thought Kellic should probably have dwelt on the former sentiment a little longer, then reminded herself that her family was in grave danger of losing both home and ship.

"There was nothing there," Lady Galanor said.

"Oh." Kellic's disappointment was almost comic.

"Fortunately, your sister has a new salvage site."

"Oh?" Kellic's brows rose. To Mirian's ears, he didn't sound as pleased as he should have.

"We're keeping the details quiet, though." Lady Galanor stepped close, and beckoned Kellic to lean forward. She spoke into his ear so that Mirian had to strain to hear. "We think we were deliberately targeted, so the location's remaining secret until after we launch."

"My goodness." He straightened and looked between Alderra and Mirian. "How soon will you leave?"

"I have to look into some things," Mirian answered. "It'll be a few days."

Rendak came up beside Mirian and saluted Kellic.

"So you didn't find anything, then," Kellic said. "Who did we lose?"

"Vemik and Alia. We're taking up a collection for their families."

Kellic nodded. "Quite right. Quite right."

With their wage-earners dead, both families would have a difficult time making ends meet. The proper thing for Kellic to do would be to hand over money immediately, but he only shook his head and fingered his cane. "I wish that we ourselves weren't so severely stretched for resources. I hope the families understand."

"Here." Mirian lifted Rendak's hand, pulled two of the three remaining emeralds from her pouch, and dropped them into his calloused palm. The moment, and Rendak's reaction, was so similar to the one that had played out with Captain Akimba that she found herself wondering about the *Red Leopard*. The ship was probably at a wharf unloading its cargo. There might even be a carriage en route to her home with her sea chest.

Rendak stared at the sparkling gems and whistled under his breath.

"Allow me, as well," Alderra Galanor said, and passed over her coin purse.

"That's very generous of you, m'lady," Kellic said with a bow.

But Lady Galanor's attention was focused only on Rendak, who inclined his head politely. "You're very kind, m'lady. Mirian, are you sure you can afford this?"

"I'll be fine," she said.

"I'll pass these on immediately." Once more Rendak bowed to Lady Galanor, then moved up the gangway after Gombe and Tokello.

"Well then." Lady Galanor indicated the wharf. "Shall we be off? It's been a long day."

"Oh, of course." Kellic indicated the exit with a sweeping bow and then followed on the heels of Lady Galanor and her son. Mirian trailed, trying not to look at the woman huddled weeping beside Alia or the two young men staring down at the other sail-wrapped body, wiping their eyes while Rendak talked seriously with them.

Tokello stepped out of the shadows and fell in step with Mirian. "Someone of sense needs to run this business." She flashed a smile. "It's good to have you back, child."

She wished it felt good to be back. "It's good to see you, Tokello."

"Wait until you see my niece. She's practically as tall as you now. And running the stables! She loves those nags. She'd sleep out there in the hay with them if I let her!"

Mirian peered past the lantern burning at the wharf's end to the ridge road and the sloped walk up to their house. She could just make out the second-story tower that jutted above the manor wall. Not so long ago her mother had routinely watched each night from its roof for the *Daughter*'s return. Had she observed them as they dropped anchor this evening?

Tokello could read her mood easily enough. "It must be a hard homecoming for you, Mirian. I'm so sorry about your father."

"Thank you."

"Death's harder on the ones left behind," she said sagely.

The sailors and salvage crew dispersed in groups, heading home in the horse-drawn carts family and friends had brought for them. Kellic had a carriage waiting for the Galanors. He offered to escort them home himself, but they demurred, and Alderra called out to Mirian that she hoped she'd be in touch soon.

Kellic stood at the end of the drive, smiling, hand raised in farewell until the carriage and carts rolled away.

Once again his eyes swept over Mirian. "Couldn't you at least have borrowed some shoes?"

"Couldn't you at least have handed over your cane? The jewels in that would have been a fine gift to the families of those dead sailors."

"I have to maintain appearances." Kellic started up the drive, punching the cane into the ground every other step, as if he actually required its use.

"Does that include potions to alter your appearance?"

His stride lagged but didn't stop. He looked over his shoulder. "Sometimes it does. Some of us have to stay and manage things."

His sharp tone was so different from what she remembered. What had happened to him? She held back from asking as she followed.

A cart came rattling down the road. She turned to see it was pulled by a swayback horse. Two men sat with the driver on the rickety bench.

"Are you coming?" Kellic called from up the drive.

The cart drew closer, slowed. The two men on the bench beside the driver were silhouetted by the sky and sea behind them, and appeared to be in conversation.

Finally the driver reined in his horse, and his head turned her way. "Pardon me, miss. I'm looking for the Raas family estate. Is this it?"

"It is."

"Oh, good."

He snapped the reins and brought the horse up the steep drive and on toward the house. Mirian stood in the grass to one side as the cart rolled up. As it came closer, she recognized her sea chest in the back. Both of the passengers stared at her, wide-eyed. "A spirit!" said the nearer. "That's her! The one who dived over the side!"

At some other time, Mirian might have had a little fun with them, but she reassured them she was flesh and blood, then tipped them a few coppers. They were still a little wary of her even after she had them carry the chest through the stout oaken door in the manor wall and onto the porch, but they promised to convey her thanks to Captain Akimba.

Kellic watched the whole thing, arms crossed.

"You should probably have had them carry it into the house for you, don't you think?"

"I can manage."

"I'll do it, then." Frowning, Kellic handed his cane off to her and bent low. He grunted in surprise as he lifted the chest.

Mirian pushed the door open and was immediately greeted with a familiar and comforting mix of scents, a blend of old wood and cooking spices and worn leather, a trace of her mother's perfume and her father's pipe smoke and a hundred other things.

"Do you carry this wherever you go?" Kellic's voice was strained.

"Not everywhere."

He moved ahead of her. "Where's this salvage drop you're taking the Galanors?"

"That's a secret."

"Don't joke, Mirian."

"I'm not joking. It must remain an absolute secret until departure time."

"I run the business now, Mirian." Kellic halted. He turned to face her as they heard the pad of slippered feet in the rooms beyond. A lantern light bobbed as someone approached them down the hallway.

"Lady Galanor has asked me to lead the expedition, Kellic. And she's sworn me to secrecy."

"I see." His tone was sharp. "So you'll simply take over, then?"

"Just this drop, Kellic. Then it's yours to run. Into the ground again, if you wish."

She wished she'd held back from the last. It had slipped out, and with a lantern suddenly shining on the both of them and the glad cry of two old servants who saw her, there was no chance to apologize. Looking at the hardened expression on her brother's face, she wasn't sure it would've done any good if she had.

Old, round-cheeked Venta squealed like a little girl and called out for Mirian's mother.

"I'll just take this back to your room." Kellic stiffly shouldered past.

Venta's husband, stooped with age, was grinning as well. Then Mirian saw her mother.

Tall, slim, garbed in an orange wrap belted in brown, she was as elegant as ever. She stared at Mirian from the courtyard archway as if she were looking at a ghost.

Odonya Raas had been just out of her teens when Leovan married her, and in her early forties she was still a handsome woman, with the slim build typical of Bas'o people. Her dark face was reminiscent of Mirian's in many ways, though rounder, softer. He full lips opened in wordless wonder, and then she beckoned her daughter into her arms. The women embraced fiercely.

Venta excused herself, saying that she'd cook something, but her precise words were lost in flood from Mirian's mother.

"Let me look at you!" Her mother held her at arm's length. "By my ancestors! Your hair's so wet. You'll ruin it if you keep it wet like that. And what is it you've come home in, child?"

"Rendak's shirt, Mother." Then she hastened to explain, lest her mother get the wrong idea about how she came to be wearing it.

They stood there in the dim entryway, lit only by the lantern Venta left them. Mirian provided an abbreviated version of her homecoming. Kellic returned near the end of the tale and waited beside their astonished mother.

"Kellic," Odonya asked. "Have you heard this?"

"Something of it."

"Now, what is with that face? Aren't you happy to see your sister?"

"Quite happy," he said with funereal dignity. "She's found a new salvage drop for us, since this one went so badly."

"Has she?"

"But she won't tell me where. She says that she's sworn to secrecy."

"Kellic," Mirian began.

"Sworn to whom?" Odonya asked.

"Lady Galanor. Mirian's going to manage things for a while." Kellic took the cane from where it was leaning against the side of the wall. "If you'll excuse me."

"Where are you going?" Odonya demanded.

"I have a few errands before a late dinner."

"No you don't." Odonya's voice was stern. "You haven't seen your sister in seven years. You're sharing a meal with her."

"I've waited seven years," Kellic said as he opened the door. "I can wait a little longer." He slammed it behind him.

Odonya sighed in disgust. "He's rushing off to that woman again."

"A girlfriend?"

"One he won't introduce me to. Well, come on then. It'll just be the two of us. Have you eaten?"

"No." She was famished, and she could already smell sizzling pork.

"You have something proper to change into?"